DEAR AS SALT

retold by
RAFE MARTIN

illustrated by
VLADYANA KRYKORKA

Scholastic Canada Ltd.

Scholastic Canada Ltd.
123 Newkirk Road, Richmond Hill, Ontario, Canada L4C 3G5

Scholastic Inc.
555 Broadway, New York, NY 10012, USA

Scholastic Australia Pty Limited
PO Box 579, Gosford, NSW 2250, Australia

Scholastic New Zealand Limited
Private Bag 94407, Greenmount, Auckland, New Zealand

Scholastic Ltd.
Villiers House, Clarendon Avenue, Leamington Spa,
Warwickshire CV32 5PR, UK

For Rose.
R.M.

For my mother, who
loved this fairy tale, and my
ancestors, for the crest.
V.K.

About the story

This version of *Dear As Salt* grew over many years, evolving as I told it to live audiences throughout North America and as far away as Japan. It is based on an old Italian folktale and owes a debt of gratitude for its initial inspiration to the version of that tale which appears in *Italian Folktales* by Italo Calvino. It will also remind knowledgeable readers of *King Lear*, but with a happy ending — and with many good meals! Stories very much like *Dear As Salt* appear in various cultures around the world. It's a universal tale, and one I'm glad to share with children today.

About the art

The illustrations for this book have a watercolour underpainting, with tempera and egg tempera finish.

Canadian Cataloguing in Publication Data

Martin, Rafe, 1946-
  Dear as salt

ISBN 0-590-74306-6 (bound) ISBN 0-590-24989-4 (pbk.)

I. Krykorka, Vladyana. II. Title.

PZ7.M36815De 1993   jC813'.54   C92-094628-3

4 3 2 1   Printed and bound in Hong Kong   7 8 9 /9

Once there was a king who had three
daughters. He also had three thrones.
He had a dark stone throne that he
sat on when he was angry. He had
a reddish wood throne that he sat
on when he was feeling
average. And when he
was feeling really
terrific, he sat on
his golden throne.

1

One day he sat himself down on the dark stone throne and called in his oldest daughter.

"Papa," she said, "you're sitting on your dark stone throne! Are you angry?"

"I am," said the king.

"Are you angry with me?" asked his daughter.

"I am!" said the king.

"But why, Papa?" she asked.

"You don't love me!" he answered.

"Oh, but I do, Papa!" she insisted.

"How much?" he asked.

And she said, "Papa, I love you as dear as bread."

The king said, "Pugh!" But, really, he was very happy. Because he knew that bread, made of wheat grown in good soil, and of dough kneaded by hand and baked in a stone oven, is filled with the power of the earth and of all growing things. So, though he said "Pugh," he was really very happy.

2

Then the king called in his second daughter. She said, "Papa, you're sitting on your dark stone throne. Are you angry?"

"I am."

"Are you angry with me?"

"I am!"

"But why, Papa?"

"Because," he answered, "you don't love me!"

"Oh, but I do, Papa!"

"How much?"

And she said, "Papa, I love you as dear as wine."

The king said, "Pugh!" But again, he was happy. He knew that to make good wine the right kind of grapes must be grown, harvested, squeezed and stored under just the right conditions. And he knew that if you are lucky, years later, when you take just a sip, your heart will feel like golden summer even on a cold, grey, winter's day. So, though he said "Pugh," he was really very happy.

3

Then he called in his youngest daughter.

She said, "Papa, you're sitting on your dark stone throne! Are you angry?"

"I am."

"Are you angry with me?"

"Yes, I am angry with you!"

"But why, Papa?"

"You don't love me!"

"But I do, Papa!"

"How much?"

And she said, "Papa, I love you as dear as salt."

When the king heard that he became furious.

"Salt?" he yelled. "Salt! Why, salt is the most common, ordinary thing. Get out of here!"

At once she ran to her mother, the queen. When the queen heard what had happened she said, "Zizola," for that was the girl's name, "the king is in one of his rages. Don't worry, I'll protect you."

And that was a good thing. For the king was so angry he called for his huntsman and said, "Go after that girl Zizola and bring me her heart, for she is a heartless girl!"

When the huntsman arrived the queen said to him, "Zizola's life is in your hands. I beg of you, the next time you go hunting bring a deer's heart to the king and tell him you have done as he ordered." And because the huntsman had a kind heart, that is what he did.

And now the king thought that Zizola was dead.

Then Zizola's mother, the queen, got a giant candlestick. There was a door in the candlestick and inside was a little bed, a night table, a chest of drawers and a bookcase with lots of books.

The queen said, "Zizola, get into the candlestick. Everything's going to be all right."

So Zizola got into the candlestick. Then her mother called for some of the men of the palace.

"Take this giant candlestick down to the market and sell it," said the queen. "If someone comes along who is cruel or greedy I don't care how much money is offered, you must say it costs a great fortune. But if someone comes along who seems kind and generous, you say it costs very little. Do you understand?"

They scratched their heads and said, "We think so, Your Highness."

And she said, "Good."

So they took that giant candlestick down to the market. Soon a rich man came riding by. He stopped his coach, tapped on the giant candlestick with his gold-headed cane, and said, "I want this giant candlestick. When people see it in my house they will all envy me. How much will you sell it for? I'll give you cash, right on the spot. So make it your best price."

They looked at one another and said, "For you? Why for you it's . . . it's five hundred chests of gold."

"Five hundred chests of gold!" exclaimed the rich man angrily. And, shouting at his coachman, he drove rapidly away.

After a time there came a prince riding on a great horse. He stopped and gazed at the giant candlestick. "This beautiful candlestick is a lovely thing," he said. "How my friends will enjoy its light on dark winter nights. I think that even the saddest person would find joy upon seeing such a candlestick. Tell me, please, how much it might cost?"

And they looked at one another and said, "For you? Why for you, it's one gold coin."

"One gold coin!" he exclaimed. "This is too good to be true! It would be a bargain at any price. Here's your money and a little something extra for you besides. My thanks!"

The prince's men carted the giant candlestick back to the palace and carried it up to the prince's rooms. Then the prince went down the spiralling stone stairs to the kitchen at the bottom of the palace. He said to the cooks, "I am going to the opera tonight. But first I will walk in my garden. After that I shall go up to my rooms, eat my dinner, and go. So bring my food up to my quarters."

The cooks said, "Of course, Your Highness."

And the prince said, "Good."

The prince went out into the garden. He sniffed the fragrant flowers and breathed the sweet air. He watched the birds soaring and looping overhead, and he watched the great, red-gold ball of the sun as it slowly set.

The cooks went up to his room, spread a fresh cloth on the table, and set out the meal. It was spaghetti with tomato sauce. It smelled delicious. They gave him a nice little salad too, a dish of grated parmesan cheese, a loaf of garlic bread, and a bottle of sparkling grape juice. Then they closed the door and left.

But what happened? As soon as they were gone, the door of the candlestick opened and out stepped Zizola. She sat down at the table and she ate and she drank until she finished it all. She wiped her lips with the linen napkin, got back into the candlestick, and closed the door.

Just then the door of the room opened and in stepped the prince. Where was his food?

He ran down the spiral stone stairs, way down to the kitchen at the bottom of the palace, and there he yelled and he shouted, "Someone has eaten my meal!"

"It wasn't us, Your Highness!" cried the cooks. "It must have been the dog or the cat. We wouldn't do such a thing."

"Well, that may be," said the prince after a moment. "Perhaps you are right. I must leave now for the opera, but I'm going out again tomorrow night. Bring my meal up to my rooms tomorrow, and this time, make sure the dog and the cat don't get in."

"Yes, Your Highness," said the cooks.

And the prince said, "Good."

The next evening, once again, the prince went out into the garden. He sniffed the fragrant flowers and breathed the sweet air. He watched the birds fly across the darkening sky and the great ball of the sun slowly set.

His cooks went up to his rooms, set out a nice tablecloth and put out a delicious meal. This second night they gave him lasagna. It smelled wonderful. Of course, they gave him another salad. They gave him another loaf of garlic bread. And tonight, so he would be in good spirits, they gave him a little bottle of wine. Then they closed the door tight, so the dog and cat couldn't get in, and they left.

As soon as they were gone, the door of the candlestick opened and out stepped Zizola. She sat down at the table and she ate and she drank until she finished it all. She wiped her lips with the linen napkin, got back into the candlestick and closed the door, just as the door of the room opened and in stepped the prince.

Oh, he was furious! He ran down to the kitchen, and he yelled and he shouted, "Someone has eaten my meal!"

The cooks cried, "It wasn't us, Your Highness! We would never do such a thing! It *must* have been the dog and the cat!"

"Really," said the prince. "Perhaps. Now listen, I'm going out again tomorrow night. I'm going to give you one last chance. This time no one is to eat my meal — or else! Do you understand?"

"Yes, Your Highness," gulped the cooks.

"Good," said the prince. And he left.

The next night, once again, the cooks went up to the prince's rooms, spread out a nice tablecloth and set out a delicious meal. This third night they gave him pizza with everything on it. It smelled delicious. They gave him another little bottle of wine and a vase with beautiful flowers. And, closing the door tight, they left. There was no way the dog and cat could get in.

But what happened? The door of the candlestick opened. Out stepped Zizola. She sat down and she ate and she ate and she drank. But what she didn't know is that that night the prince was hiding under the table. As Zizola ate he stuck out his head. He looked her in the face. His heart began to beat faster. He fell in love with Zizola!

The prince got out from under the table. "My dear girl," he said, "what were you doing in that gigantic candlestick?" So Zizola told him the whole story — how she had told her father, the king, she loved him dear as salt; how he had been so angry; and how her mother, the queen, had put her in the giant candlestick to save her life.

"Don't worry," said the prince. "It's going to be all right." Then they ate and they talked, they laughed and they sang and they danced. Late that night Zizola got back into her candlestick. In the morning, the prince went down the spiral stone stairs to the kitchen and said to the cooks, "Now that . . . "

"Y-e-s, Your Highness," said the cooks, their knees knocking together with fright.

"Why, that was a very good meal you gave me last night," said the prince.

"Oh, thank you, Your Highness," exclaimed the cooks in relief. "We are so glad to hear it!"

"Now," said the prince, "I'm going to be busy for the next three days. I'm going to be hungry, too. Send all my meals up to my rooms. And make them double portions, will you? You know, enough for two."

"Certainly, Your Highness," said the cooks. "With pleasure."

And the prince said, "Good."

For three days Zizola and the prince ate and talked. They laughed and sang and danced. After three days the prince came back down those spiralling stone stairs, went to his mother and said, "Mama, I'm getting married."

"That's wonderful!" said the queen. "Who are you going to marry?"

"Mama," he said, "I'm going to marry the candlestick."

"No!" she exclaimed in shock, "you can't marry a candlestick!"

"Mama," he said, "I'll marry the candlestick or I'll marry no one."

What could the poor woman do?

The men of the palace carried the candlestick down the spiralling stairs. They put it in a carriage. The prince sat next to the candlestick, put his arm around the candlestick, and off they drove to the church. His men carried the candlestick inside and set it before the altar. The prince stood there looking so happy. His mother sat in the corner, crying bitterly.

The priest came in and began to read the marriage ceremony. Just as he got to the part where he was about to pronounce them man and . . . candlestick, the little door opened and out stepped Zizola! She looked beautiful. When the queen saw that her son was marrying the girl in the candlestick, not the candlestick itself, she became so happy she began to laugh and cry at the same time.

29

When the wedding was over she rushed to Zizola and said, "My dear girl, what were you doing in that gigantic candlestick?"

So Zizola told her the whole story — how she had told her father, the king, she loved him dear as salt; how he had been so angry; and how her mother, the queen, had put her in the giant candlestick to save her life.

"Don't worry," said the prince's mother. "You are safe with us, dear Zizola."

"Yes," said Zizola. "And I am very happy. Still, if you are willing to help me, I think that together we can fix it all."

"Of course, dear," said both the prince and the queen. "Certainly we shall help." So Zizola told them her plan.

The next day, the queen threw a big dinner party. She invited all the kings and queens, the princes and princesses of the neighbouring provinces to come celebrate the wedding.

Before the guests arrived, she went down to the kitchen and said to the cooks, "You are the best cooks in all the land."

"Thank you, Your Highness."

"And tonight," the queen continued, "I want you to do something special. Tonight I want you to make sure there is no salt in the food you serve Zizola's father."

"But Your Highness!" exclaimed the cooks in dismay. "We can't do that! He will think that we are terrible cooks."

"Let the king think what he will," answered the queen.

And, because she was the queen, the poor cooks could only say, "Yes, Your Highness."

And the queen said, "Good."

That night, when the guests arrived, the queen made sure that Zizola's father was seated right next to her. She clapped her hands. "Bring out the meal," she called. And the cooks entered the dining hall carrying big plates of soup. It was minestrone, and it smelled delicious! The guests took up their royal spoons and began to eat, saying, "Marvelous! Delicious! Fantastic! The best soup we've ever had!"

All except Zizola's father. He took a sip. His face curled in distaste. He took another. He looked even worse. Then he put his spoon down.

"What's the matter?" asked the queen. "Don't you like the cooking?"

"I do, Your Highness," he answered. "I just want to leave room for the rest of the meal."

"That's good," she said, "because there's plenty." She clapped her hands again.

Again the cooks entered the hall, this time carrying big platters of food. It was eggplant parmigiana and it too smelled delicious! Once again the guests were served. They took up their royal knives and their royal forks and they began to eat, saying, "Delicious! Terrific! Fantastic! The best eggplant parmigiana we've ever had!"